Betsy Blu
and the Great Sport Revolution

Danielle Oultram
Illustrated by Jessica Corlett

For my girls Pearl and Primrose,

May you always feel the strength to be true to yourselves.

Betsy Blu was nearly two and a girl quite like you,
Each day full with all things exciting and new,
Weekends sunny and bright with many an adventure,
Clipping on her helmet, into the forest they would venture.

With Daddy pedaling, their bike was fast,
Laughing and waving as the world flew past.
Fairy hunts and feeding the ducks,
Twilight adventures and sunsets they would look.

The day had come when she would no longer fit,
Outgrowing the seat on Daddy's bike she would sit,
The day of her birthday and quite a surprise,
All wrapped up, her own bike to ride.

Decorated with a bow with her name on too,
Cherry red with stars that were blue,
Handle bar tassels of blue satin ribbon,
A basket on the front to keep her treasures hidden.

6

With pads on knees and her helmet on ready,
“Ok Betsy Blu, slow down, just go steady!”
With Daddy running along, he cautiously let go,
Ready to catch with tears in full flow.
Nervous excitement was thick in the air,
A memory they would forever share,
Riding her bike, the world opened up,
Twists and turns, at every path she took.

A ball of energy, Betsy was always on the go,
Out and about until daylight was low.
Looking at the world through eyes full of wonder,
A joyful child, others longed to join her.

Freckles on her nose and a head full of curls,
"You should be on a stage my girl",
Confused and bewildered, Betsy would frown,
The comment was made from a shopkeeper in town,
"Absolutely not!" she would shout with a stomp,
Returning to her bike without a prompt.

SHOP

Now Betsy was six and surrounded by friends,
Tiaras, ball gowns and castles, playground games would depend,
Along she would play, at ease in the moment,
However, curiosity was building for another component.

No longer would Betsy stay trapped in the castle,
"I'll find an escape route, it's really no hassle!"
Kicking off the slippers and back in her trainers,
"Watch me go" she shouted to her princess neighbours,
Skipping and cartwheeling she navigated through,
An unusual princess was Betsy Blu.

One Sunday afternoon whilst sheltering from the rain,
The Olympics on the TV screen - "Betsy! Do I have to ask again?"
Her gaze was fixed, everything else was distant,
"A girl with golden hair who was absolutely brilliant"
Riding her bike as fast as can be,
Up and down ramps, as high as a tree,
Standing, twirling and upside down,
Dancing in the air, the wheels landing safely on the ground.
Her, I want to be her,
Betsy's thoughts began to stir.

BMX
Finals

Winter had passed with the first signs of spring,
At home with Daddy, she heard the telephone ring,
"Betsy Blu come and join us at the park" said Josie from school,
"Bring your tiara, it is going to be cool!"
With a skip and a hop, on her bike she went,
Taking the long way round she was most content.

Arriving at the park she set her bike down,
“Betsy over here, up the tower” said the girl in the crown,
Running to join them, thoughts of being chased by a dragon,
Unbeknown to her that something magic was to happen.
At the highest point, came a distraction from the game,
The jumps and the ramps calling her name,
A BMX track like the one on the television,
Could she be dreaming she eyed with suspicion.
Now tall enough to see, over the fields she could look,
A beautiful view like the one in her book.

“Betsy come on, it’s time for the dance”
But still she stood eyes fixed in a trance,
“Let’s go there” to her friends she pointed,
They turned to look as it all became disjointed,
“Us girls belong here, in the castle we wait,
To be rescued by a prince is our fate”.

Betsy was torn, she faced a dilemma,
Would she have to be a princess forever?
She looked at her friends, then again at the track,
Vowing one day that she would come back.
As her eyes looked away,
A princess she would play,
But this Saturday at the park,
Could this be the start?

Tucked up in bed, as the light turned out,
Betsy grew sleepy and wondered what it was all about.
Dreaming of pedaling fast and gliding through the air,
A sense of freedom with the wind in her hair.
In the morning she woke determined to be heard,
Today was the day and she would not be deterred.
Step by step, she knew what to do,
She had to move quick this was true.

Bursting in to the kitchen, he jumped with a fright,
“Daddy I have an idea, it came to me last night,
Get on your helmet and pump up those tyres,
We are off to the BMX track to join the flyers!”

The car was packed, bikes on the roof,
Betsy looked across, Daddy's smile as proof,
Her wheels would touch the concrete, today was the day,
With him by her side, she knew it would be okay.

As they arrived with butterflies in her tummy,
Daddy passed Betsy her bike, "let's go buddy".
Sat on her bike, it felt like home,
Through the golden gates, like she had always known.

On top of the ramp, at the edge she did wait,
Was this too big for a girl who is eight?
Betsy closed her eyes, like a bird in the sky,
It was now or never, here goes her first try,
With a one….two….three, she was free!
Down the ramps and around the bends,
A smile on her face with no thought of her friends.
Daddy cheered on as the hours slipped by,
Eyes glistening like diamonds in the sky.

Confidence was high, self-belief like no other,
Holding on tight, one ramp after another,
When Betsy lined up for the jump,
Up in the air and down with a thump,
The bike went crash, with cuts on knees,
To the bottom she slid, Daddy running to cuddle and squeeze,
"A real BMX racer - what a big first crash,
Up you get poppet, quick as a flash".
Helped to her feet with the power of a plaster,
Ready to go again but this time faster!

The sun was setting and tummies began to rumble,
It was time to leave but on this she did not stumble,
Was this where she was supposed to have been?
Thoughts returning of the television screen,
“One day it will be me as the wheels leave the ground,
Cheers will be heard from all around”.
A dream was decided before she was ten,
Underlined in her diary with her best marker pen.

The days passed by, thoughts at the Tabletop,
The kicks and the flips over the rollers she would hop,
One day on the ramps she heard but a whisper,
To the castle she turned, as the sound grew crisper,
"What will they think of me with no crown in sight?"
Looking to the girls, her heart grew tight.
"Go Betsy Blu!" she heard the girls cry,
Her wheels took flight as she faced up to the sky,
Twisting in the air, she landed the jump,
The girls cheered, what a triumph!

A real inspiration, a lot can be learned,
Following her heart to happiness was confirmed,
Life is not set with pathways defined,
Listen to the messages within your own mind.
Remember Betsy Blu and her BMX dream,
When things become confusing and not as they seem,
Be brave and be bold,
For your story is about to be told.

Printed in Great Britain
by Amazon

79069332R00022